Polly Pomegranate

Delia Damson

Belinda Blackcurrant

Alice Apple

Peter Potato

Wee Willie Water Melon

D0522149

The Garden Gang
Stories and pictures by
Jayne Fisher

Other Garden Gang stories

Series 793

First Edition

Oscar Orange

Ladybird Books Loughborough

Oscar Orange
was handsome,
well-dressed,
intelligent, successful
and fearless!
Everyone liked him.
He lived in a big
house and should
have been very happy.
But he was not
and the reason
for this was that
he was terribly small.

His friends said,
"What does it matter
if you are small?
It doesn't make
you any less handsome
or clever!"
But Oscar
secretly worried
about his height
and decided that
before another year
had passed he would
have grown five
centimetres taller.
He thought about it
all the time and made
secret plans.

First he tried
eating more and
drinking lots of milk.
But although this made
him stronger
and perhaps a little
fatter he did not
grow one tiny bit taller.
His belt felt rather tight
and uncomfortable,
so he had to give up
over-eating.

Then he had
another brilliant idea.
If he hung
from a bough
of the apple tree
for an hour each day,
he would be
sure to stretch.
Poor Oscar!
He only became
very red in the face
and got large
blisters on his hands.

"I know,"
thought Oscar
one evening
while he was
sitting at supper,
"plants grow well
in manure.
Why shouldn't I?"
So early the next
morning, before anyone
was about, he crept
up to Mr Rake's
manure heap and
carefully filled his shoes.
"Now I'll really grow,"
he said.

What a smell!
Penelope Strawberry
put her lace
handkerchief over
her nose as she
hurried by.
The pea twins
were nearly sick
and Alice Apple
hurriedly climbed
to the top of her tree
as Oscar passed
beneath her.
Even the birds and
insects avoided him.

"Whatever does he think he's up to?" cried Patrick Pear, holding his breath as he tried to fish in a plastic bucket. In fact all the Garden Gang agreed that he smelt horrid and wondered how they could tell him without hurting his feelings. "It's really too bad of him," they said.

But they were even
more alarmed
when they saw
what he did next.
He filled a large
watering can and
began to pour
the cold water
all over himself.
"Whatever are
you doing?" they
all shouted.
"I'm growing!"
replied Oscar
with a smile.
But was he?

Oscar
stood dripping
onto the floor as
Mark Marrow
brought out a ruler
to measure him.
And do you know,
he had not grown
one tiny bit.
He burst into floods of
tears and sat
sobbing in the grass.
How sad they
all were to see him
so upset.

"You really don't
need to be tall
to be well liked
and successful,"
said Peter Potato.
"But if that's what
you want, I
suppose we can
think of something.
In fact I have
rather a good idea."
As you know
Peter Potato
was very good at
making things and
away he went
to his shed.

Peter soon reappeared
carrying a pair of
very special shoes.
They were big and
black and shiny.
Oscar put them on
and smartly strutted
across the garden.
Everyone cheered and
felt pleased as they
saw his happy
smiling face.
At last his secret
wish had been granted.
He had become . . .

five centimetres taller!

Augustus Aubergine

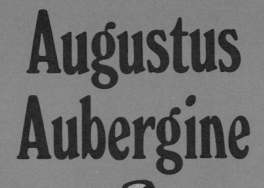

Augustus was a
cute little Aubergine.
His family had
brought him over
from Rome, in Italy,
when he was a baby.
He lived by the
fountain in a little
stone house, which
he called his villa,
and he always wore
a Roman toga and
sandals because
it made him feel
important.

Mind you,
he was not
very often seen
during the daytime
and the Garden Gang
thought him
a little odd. In fact
they thought him
rather mysterious
because he was often
to be seen prowling
about after dark
and many of the
Garden Gang children
said that he was a
magician.

"Perhaps he's shy,"
said Roger Radish,
remembering the days
when he used to hide
from everyone.
"Oh, I don't think so,"
said Pam Parsnip,
"I once met him when
I was out walking
in the woods
and I found him
perfectly charming.
He's such a gentleman."

They became more
curious when they
passed his house
each day and heard
him snoring inside.
"Why doesn't he come
out in the daytime, like
everyone else?"
they thought.
"I don't know how
he can bear to miss the
fresh air and sunshine,"
said Bertie
Brussels Sprout,
who was always doing
keep fit exercises.

Then came the
tapping noises.
Every evening and
sometimes through
the night, the sound of
tapping and hammering
was heard coming from
Augustus' garden.
This went on for weeks.
No one dared to ask
him what he was doing.
They all decided to
peep through his
hedge one evening
after dark.
It would be fun.

tap
t
tap

tap
tap
tap
tap
tap

37

All the next day,
the excitement in
the garden grew.
Fruit and vegetable
people were seen in
small groups talking or
whispering together.
They could hardly
wait for the evening
to come and the
great adventure they
felt sure they were
going to have.
Why did Augustus
sleep through the day
and work at night?

That night it really
was funny to see all
the Garden Gang
creeping along in
the dark behind
Augustus Aubergine's
garden hedge.
Of course the pea
twins managed to fall
over each other,
and everyone,
including the strict
Gertrude Gooseberry,
began to giggle.
People always start
to giggle when they
try to be serious.

How they giggled!
First it was softly and
then it grew louder
and louder, ending up
with them all
rolling about in
the grass, holding
their sides.
Augustus Aubergine
peered through
his hedge in
astonishment.
He could hardly believe
his eyes.
"Do come into my
garden," he said shyly,
and in they all tramped.

"I'm so glad you've come," he said. "There is something special I would like you to see." He asked them to follow him and led them to a small round building he had built. It had a glass top, rather like a bubble. "This is my observatory," he said. "You may slide back the top and take a look, one at a time."

Inside was a massive
telescope and each
one in turn was
allowed to look
through the eye piece
and peer into the
night sky.
So this is why he
came out at night!
He watched the stars.
Augustus explained
all the things they
could see and their
eyes grew wide with
wonder.

They saw mountains
on the moon; Jupiter with
its multi-coloured bands
and four bright moons;
Saturn with its rings;
galaxies with spirals
and balls of millions
of stars and glowing
patches of multi-
coloured gas.
They were
fascinated and now
they realised that
their mysterious
Augustus
Aubergine was . . .

a great astronomer!

Paul Pumpkin

Bertie Brussels Sprout

Mark Marrow

Gertrude
Gooseberry

Tim Tomato

Patrick Pear

Avril Apricot